Fantastic Fairy Tales

PINOCCHIO

An imprint of Om Books International

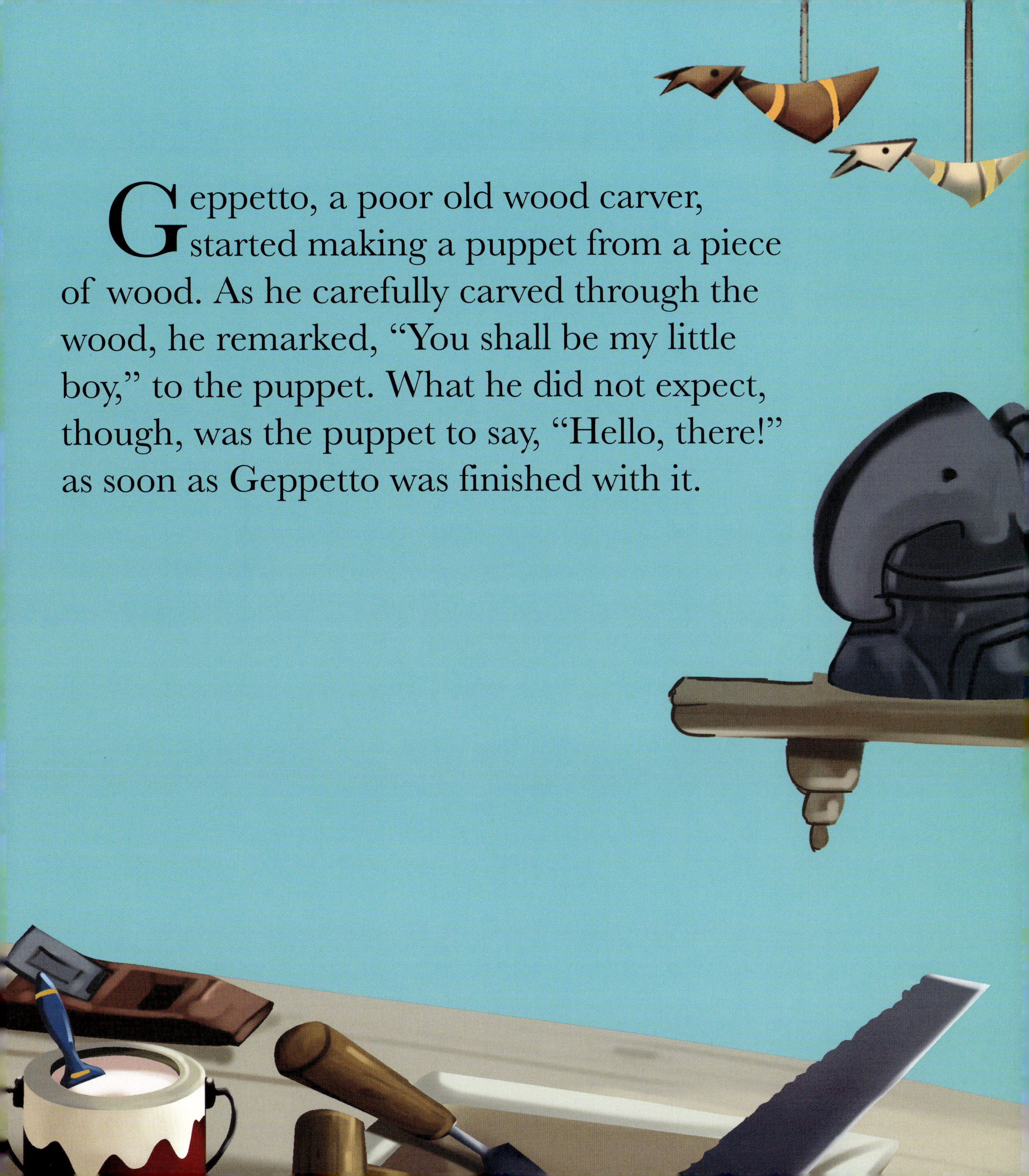

Geppetto, a poor old wood carver, started making a puppet from a piece of wood. As he carefully carved through the wood, he remarked, "You shall be my little boy," to the puppet. What he did not expect, though, was the puppet to say, "Hello, there!" as soon as Geppetto was finished with it.

Needless to say, Geppetto was extremely surprised. He had not expected a puppet made of wood to speak. "How on earth did you do that?" asked a bewildered Geppetto.

The puppet had more to say to that. "You gave me a mouth and therefore I can speak. I can do a lot more than just talk." And so saying, the puppet started to dance, throwing its hands and legs in the air.

Geppetto was indeed very impressed by his creation. He named the puppet Pinocchio and decided that Pinocchio would go to school and learn with all the other children.

The next day, Pinocchio waved goodbye to Geppetto as he left for school. However, even before he could get there, Pinocchio stopped to see a puppet show at the fair.

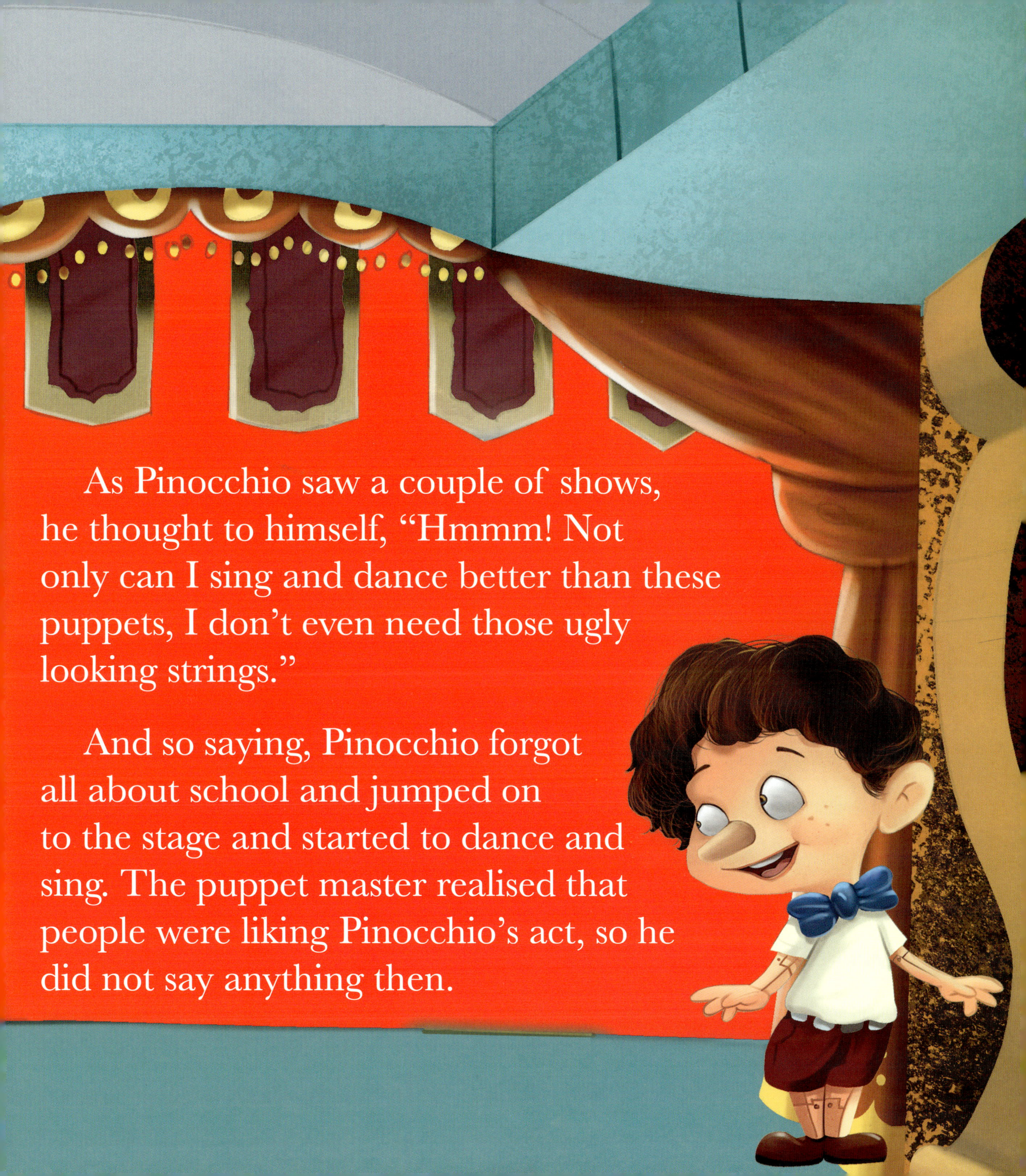

As Pinocchio saw a couple of shows, he thought to himself, "Hmmm! Not only can I sing and dance better than these puppets, I don't even need those ugly looking strings."

And so saying, Pinocchio forgot all about school and jumped on to the stage and started to dance and sing. The puppet master realised that people were liking Pinocchio's act, so he did not say anything then.

But as soon as the show was over, he caught Pinocchio by his nose and threw him off the stage, warning him, "Don't ever come back here. You're just a puppet, not a real boy!"

Pinocchio was naturally very upset. He sobbed and sobbed. “What does the puppet master think of himself? I am just like a real boy!” Pinocchio reasoned with himself.

Suddenly, Pinocchio saw a pink fairy come before him. “Who are you?” asked a surprised Pinocchio.

The fairy smiled and replied, “I am your Guardian Fairy, Pinocchio. I saw you crying and so I came to pay you a visit. How was school today?”

Pinocchio kept a straight face and said, "School was fun. I learnt quite a lot today."

No sooner did Pinocchio say this, his nose jumped up and grew a little longer. Pinocchio tried pressing on his nose, but it just did not come back in. He looked with surprise at his Guardian Fairy.

“What is happening? Why is my nose growing like this?” asked a surprised Pinocchio. His Guardian Fairy replied, “Every time you tell a lie, dear Pinocchio, your nose will grow like this. And every time you speak the truth, it will go back inside the same distance.”

But Pinocchio was adamant. “I did not lie even once. I did indeed go to school,” cried the little puppet boy. And even as he finished speaking, his nose grew longer.

Pinocchio's Guardian Fairy then said, "You must stop lying, Pinocchio. Now go home and remember, you will turn into a real boy only if you are brave and honest. So never tell lies again and always try to be honest and brave." So saying, his Guardian Fairy left.

Pinocchio decided to go back home to Geppetto. But as he was walking past the beach, he saw the same puppet master walking along the sea shore. Seeing Pinocchio walk towards him again, the angry puppet master grabbed his hand, and threw poor Pinocchio into the sea!

Even before Pinocchio knew what was happening, a giant whale came and gobbled him up. As Pinocchio landed in the whale's belly, he felt someone's breath on him.

"Who are you?" screamed Pinocchio.

“Pinocchio, is that you?” asked the other person in return. It was Geppetto! He had been looking for Pinocchio when Pinocchio didn’t return from school, and was washed away into the sea by a big wave and then swallowed by a whale.

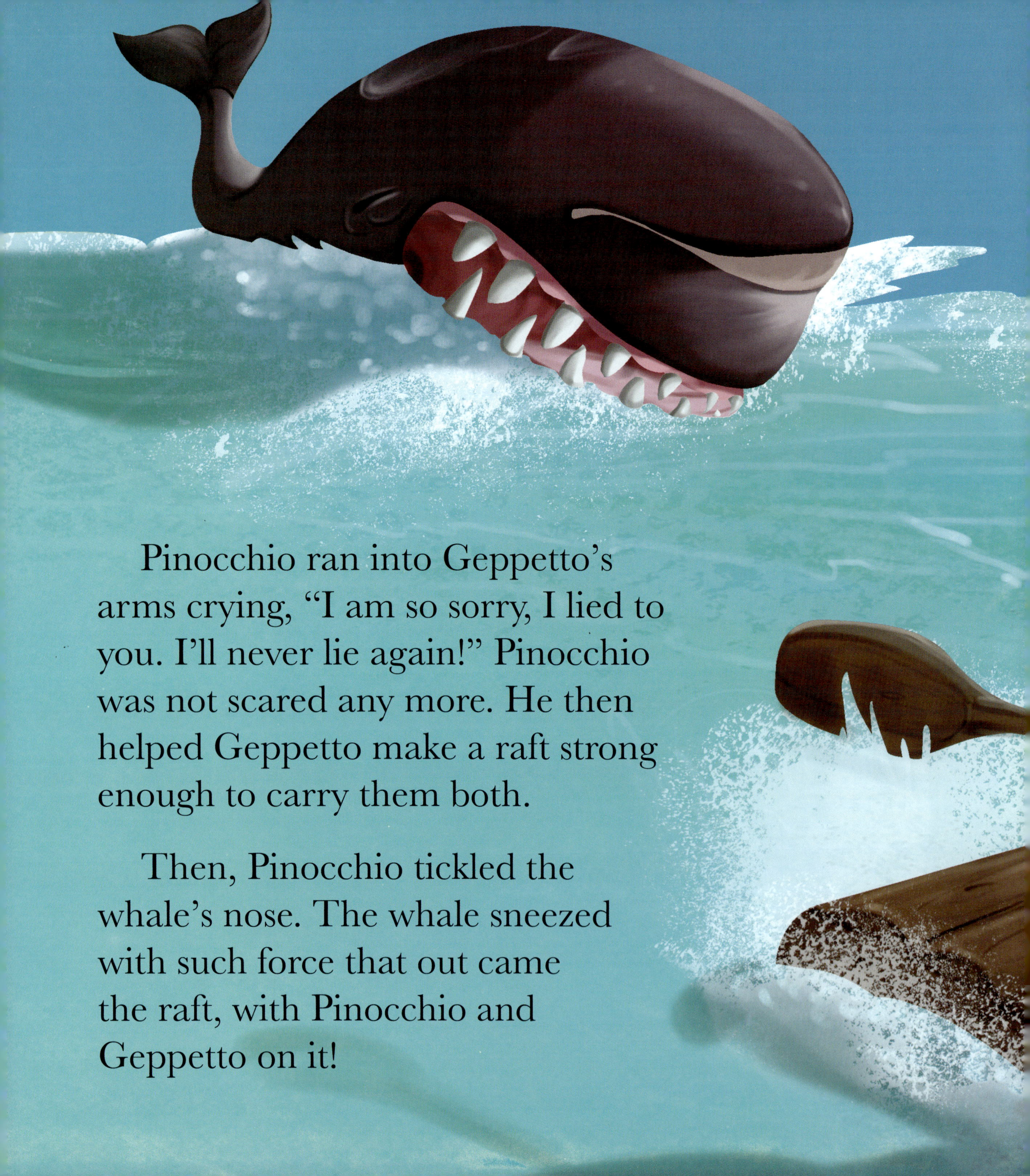

Pinocchio ran into Geppetto's arms crying, "I am so sorry, I lied to you. I'll never lie again!" Pinocchio was not scared any more. He then helped Geppetto make a raft strong enough to carry them both.

Then, Pinocchio tickled the whale's nose. The whale sneezed with such force that out came the raft, with Pinocchio and Geppetto on it!

Finally, Geppetto and Pinocchio were on their way home, rowing with great speed over the choppy waves. That night, as Geppetto tucked Pinocchio into bed, he said, "You are my son, and I shall always love you.

Today you have been brave and honest, Pinocchio, and I hope you grow up just like this." Pinocchio remembered what his Guardian Fairy had said to him. As he drifted off to sleep, Pinocchio wondered whether her words would ever come true.

Next morning, as Geppetto got out of bed, he saw Pinocchio come running towards him, yelling. "Look Father, I am a real boy!"

Geppetto hugged Pinocchio lovingly and thanked God for giving him such a wonderful son.